Anne Rooney does not eat meat, in case the taste of blood becomes too appealing.

When not writing books she haunts the cemeteries and catacombs of Paris and Venice and raises non-vampiric daughters and chickens in Cambridge. She studied at a haunted college and her first car was a haunted van; the undead hold no fears for her.

With thanks to Kate and Hannah Frew, Mary Hoffman, Shahrukh Husain, Harriet Riley and Andrew Laws (@Andrew_Culture).

Life Sucks

by Anne Rooney
www.annerooney.co.uk

Published by Ransom Publishing Ltd.
Radley House, 8 St. Cross Road, Winchester, Hants.
SO23 9HX, UK
www.ransom.co.uk

ISBN   978 184167 298 4

First published in 2012

Life Sucks

ANNE ROONEY

Ransom

Hungary, August ...

Juliette, Omar, Finn, Ruby and Alistair find a dead body in the forest ...

... Twenty-four hours later, they tie the murderer, Ava, to a tree, as one by one they fall sick ...

... When they wake, they are vampires, and that murderer looks rather appealing ...

... Mysterious nobleman Ignace, 400 years old and more sophisticated than is good for him, prevents them snacking on her ...

... But that dead body isn't as dead as it looked ...

... They go to Ignace's castle for a crash-course in being a modern vampire.

And so their adventures begin.

This is Finn's story ...

One

The sound of crunching bones set Finn's teeth on edge. He could have coped with the rest – at least until the lunatic slurped the marrow from the cracked bones. But that splintering sound – it just wasn't good.

'Cut it out, dude!' Finn called from the window. The figure below carried on crunching and slurping.

'What are you eating, anyway?' he asked. 'Is it human?'

'No. Eez cow. Much trouble if I eat human persons.'

'Do you have a name?' Finn asked. 'Do you remember it?'

'My name eez Lorenzo.' He made a sucking noise. Finn didn't like to imagine what he was sucking.

'That's disgusting, man! Do you have to?'

Lorenzo carried on with his meal.

'How long are you going to be following me around? I don't need a minder – especially not a mad, cow-sucking minder.'

'You do,' Lorenzo said through a mouthful of flesh. 'Mister Ignace, he say I have to look after you. You are Finn Casey, yes? I have right vampire? He say I am a good one for you because you and me, we are both mad. Eez funny, no? He thinks you as mad as me!'

'No, it's not funny, it's a right insult! I'm not as mad as you – you're a screwball cow-sucker and I'm just angry. Will you be following me home? My mam's not going to be too pleased if I turn up with a mad vampire in tow.'

'But you are mad vampire also. She not so pleased with that, eh? Lady have two mad vampires when she expected none. Eez big shock for her, no?'

Finn slammed the window. He had one more night in the hostel. The others had gone. After the disastrous camping trip, Ignace had taken them to his castle for a crash course in being a vampire. He had sent Ava away after a day as she wasn't a vampire, but the others he had kept for a week. He let them go just before they were due to go home. Juliette had taken a first-class flight to Heathrow as soon as they got back to Budapest – she didn't even wait for the flight she was booked on. Omar, Ruby and Alistair had flown to Luton a few hours ago – they'd have landed by now. His own flight was tomorrow.

And so Finn was now alone in a ropey hostel in Budapest, except for this wild lunatic Lorenzo. Ignace had taken charge of Juliette himself – no surprise there; you could see him drooling over her perfect, rich-girl beauty. The 400-year-old nobleman and the super-model – what fun the papers would have with that if it came out. And Finn had ended up with this freak Lorenzo as his mentor. Or minder.

Finn would have liked to go with Ruby. She was

his kind of girl. Sparky, hard, not scared to stand up for herself. But she had that dorky brother, Alistair; that was a hassle. He was always hanging around, always being an idiot, counting things, obsessing about stupid stuff. But Ruby, with her spiky hair and strong body – not scrawny like that spoilt brat of a model – Ruby was cool.

A bone hit the window.

'Hey, I have to look after you. What are you doing, new boy?'

Finn dragged his T-shirt off and lay on the narrow bed in his jeans. He reached over to turn off the light.

'I'm going to sleep. Shut up.'

'Mister Ignace, he say you have to eat the ProVamp capsules, so you don't want the blood. You done that? Or you want to come hunt cows with me?'

'Why would I hunt cows? Especially with you?'

'Nice juicy cow, full of good blood. They do not run fast. Eez easy to catch. A cow lasts some days. Eez more tasty than capsules.'

'Are you seriously suggesting I run around Hungary with a wild, mad vampire sucking cows? How on earth did this happen to my life?'

'You were bited, Mister Ignace say, by vampired mosquito.'

'Yes, I know *how* it happened. What I mean is – oh, never mind. I don't want any cows. Feel free to eat them all yourself. I'm going to sleep.'

Two

Finn turned the amp to maximum and blasted the house with sound. He'd been home two weeks and was working on a new song. It totally possessed him, driving everything else from his mind as he tried to fit the chords to the words, the words to his thoughts. It was nearly there.

The house shook with the music – it was too small to contain it. He imagined the walls filling up with sound, something like the ringing he had in his ears after a loud session.

Soon, his sister would be home and he'd have to turn it down. His half-sister. He didn't want to be linked with her. She was everything he hated, and more. She liked ponies, mermaids, pink dresses. She was eight. She had a pink bicycle and played with Barbies. She had something wrong with her that he didn't like to think about because it made him feel bad, probably something related to her father being a half-wit crack-head. At least *he* wasn't around any more.

Finn had not wanted there to be any baby. But if there had to be a baby, he'd wanted a brother. Not Gina. His anger fuelled his songs. It made them sharp and loud, witty and spiky. It gave them edge and made them work. But now he had something else to make them work. Now he was a vampire. He wouldn't just be stuck on YouTube – he'd get gigs, sell tracks, be a hit. How could he fail? He had what no one else had. This was going to be his break-out track.

Half three. He packed up his guitar and amp and dragged them to college. His sixth-form college, where he came to be humiliated by teachers who knew he didn't care about his exams. But there were recording studios there, and the video suite. After the school day, they could use the practice suites – it was worth staying for.

The rest of the band turned up: Joe and Iman on their bikes, Ellie on her scooter. Only Gray and Finn walked. They were the poor ones.

They hardly spoke as they set up, fingers working quickly to plug in leads, adjust settings, fix the mike in the practice suite. And in minutes they were playing Finn's new song, *Life Sucks*.

Finn's voice was acid, toxic. It fought with the guitar chords. It sounded yellow – wasp-yellow. All the time he stared at Ellie. Much as she liked him, it put her on edge. That look didn't seem like routine teenage lust – something else was going on, she was sure. The song finished and Finn took a gulp of water.

'Pretty good,' Gray said. He worked the sound, as well as playing drums. 'Once more. Then we'll have something I can mix.'

They played again, letting the last chord die long and slow.

'It's good, Finn,' Ellie said. 'You've really spiced it up since last week. But where did it come from?

It's not your usual stuff.'

'Well, I'm a vampire,' Finn said, baring his teeth. 'Didn't I tell you?'

She laughed. 'Well, if being a vampire means you write like this, long may it last.'

'Were you always a vampire?' Gray asked. 'Tell us, Mr Casey, when did you first discover you were a vampire?' He held the mike out to Finn in mock-interview style.

Finn pushed the mike away. He didn't laugh, but they were used to his moodiness. It went with the creative territory, he always said. But it was just his crappy life. There wasn't much to laugh about. Some people managed to laugh anyway, but not Finn.

'So,' Ellie said. 'We make the video tomorrow in the double free after the Media Studies guys get out of the video studio?'

Finn nodded, collected his kit and left without speaking to any of them. They watched him leave and Ellie went to follow, but Gray did a thumbs-down sign.

'Back off. He's got one of his strops on.'

Finn heard them as the door swung shut behind him, but didn't respond. What did he care if they thought him a pain, as long as the band worked? He was the talent, no doubt about that. But he needed a band, and for now they were good enough.

Three

Ellie had draped the studio in black fabric from Textiles and made some props in Art. She'd written a script for the video, showing how the shots broke down to match the song, and she'd put the timings alongside.

They'd shoot it four times, with three cameras, and they should get enough decent footage to put something together. There were only two characters on screen to start with – Finn as the vampire and

Ellie as the victim.

'Goth or Emo?' Finn asked Ellie, as she stretched to pin the fabric, her ripped tights laddering even more.

'I guess undead,' she answered, blowing him a kiss. Her lips were blood-red, her eyes thickly lined with black eyeliner and her face powder-white. She picked up a pouch of fake blood, dark and slightly gluey, and squished it between her fingers.

'We don't have to do the real thing, right? You aren't really going to bite me, are you?' She pouted, jutting out a fat sliver of pink lip, then laughed.

Finn felt a shudder of excitement just at the thought. He pretended it was disgust and shook his shoulders.

'Uh, no. Fake is fine.' He felt himself blush and turned away from her. He hated blushing. It wasn't easy to look hard if you blushed.

If only, he thought. He reached into his pocket and closed his fingers around the ProVamp capsule he kept there. God, if just thinking about blood gave him a rush like this, what would it be like if he really bit her? He felt his face getting hot again at the thought, and he tried to blot it from his mind. What if she noticed? But the more he looked at Ellie's smooth, white neck the worse it got. What's more, she'd let him – he knew she would.

They'd had a thing, for a while, Finn and Ellie. He'd dumped her when she got too serious. She still liked him. The band situation was tricky, but they both knew it was professional. It had to be done, and it was usually OK. But if he bit her ...

God, he wanted to bite her.

They did three run-throughs without incident. He stalked her, stage-vampire style, very camp, very over-the-top. He cornered her, wrapped her in his cloak (borrowed from Drama), sunk his (plastic) teeth into her neck and finally drank her (fake) blood as she swooned in his arms.

It was the last take that did for him.

As Ellie spun round, she grazed her hand against the sand stuck to one of the pillars of the vampire's castle. She lifted her hand to suck it away, and Finn leapt at her.

'Don't waste it!' he cried, snatching her hand. She laughed, and smeared the blood on her neck. A tiny spot, that was all it was. But he was there, on her in an instant. He fell on her neck, sucking hard, his tongue searching for all of it, every cell. It was sharp and metallic in his mouth, like tacks. He sucked so hard he thought he could taste her flowing blood beneath the skin. Surely that wasn't possible? He sucked so hard, and his hands held her so tightly, that she screamed and struggled and hit out, trying to push him away.

'Get off me!' Ellie shouted.

'Hey, man, that's enough!' Joe said. 'Take it easy!'

But Finn kept his arms wrapped around Ellie as though to protect her. Joe grabbed the crucifix they'd kept for the chapel scene – the scene Finn had refused to do – and touched it to Finn's shoulder.

'Whoa, vampire – scary crucifix coming! Come

on mate, let her go.'

Finn's head spun round and he glowered at Joe, then raised one arm over his face. Ellie broke free and ran.

'Take it away, man. I meant no harm. Don't hurt me,' Finn pleaded.

Joe stared at him, puzzled.

'It's all right, I'm not going to hurt you! But you went way too far, mate. You don't really need to scare her, OK?'

'I'm sorry, all right? I don't know what happened. I just got carried away. It was – I don't know. I don't feel too good.' He fumbled in his pocket, found the ProVamp, pulled it out and swallowed it.

'Take it easy, right? What's that you're taking? No drugs, that was the deal.'

Finn shrugged.

'Headache pill. I'm sorry, all right? Please – put that away. Don't bring it near me.'

'This?' Joe held up the crucifix and Finn flinched. 'What's the problem? I'm not going to hit you. It's only a cross.'

'Please.' It was a word Finn rarely used. Joe laughed.

'Hey, Joe.' Iman moved forward and took the cross from him. 'His mum's a Catholic. He probably doesn't like you messing with the holy stuff. Best put it down.'

Iman leaned the cross against the wall. 'I think

we'll work with what we've got now. OK, Gray?'

'Sure,' said Gray. 'There's some great stuff here – especially that last bit.'

'You *using* that?' asked Finn.

'Why not? It's good. You got any problem with it, Ellie?' She shook her head, one hand still at her neck.

'Use it. No problem. But no re-takes, OK? Vampire nutter.' She stuck her tongue out at Finn, mocking.

Finn looked at the back of her hand, the spots of red. He felt a slight desire, nothing more. The ProVamp had done its job, he'd just taken it too late. *Useful lesson*, he thought, curling his hand into a fist in his pocket.

four

Two days later, Gray posted the video on YouTube. He'd done a good job, but Finn felt uncomfortable sitting in his bedroom and watching his own frenzy, seeing Ellie's real terror.

Everyone thought it was good acting. Only he knew how real it was. It could so easily have got out of hand if Joe hadn't pounced. He saw why Ignace insisted on the ProVamp.

The video had been up only two hours, but it had already got 1,000 hits and 324 'likes'. Finn punched the air.

'Yes!'

He propped his feet on the desk and played the video again. The toolbar icon for iVamp showed he had messages, but he didn't care. It was probably Ignace trying to check up on him. He didn't want Ignace or Lorenzo bugging him all the time.

Not that Lorenzo used iVamp, or even had a computer or a phone. The man was a joke. The very thought of Lorenzo's brown, leathery skin and his scraggy, matted hair tangling around his shoulders made Finn want to laugh.

The video ended, but the room wasn't silent. There was a noise, some kind of scratching. Like fingernails on a window, Finn thought, but his bedroom was on the first floor.

He pulled the curtain aside, then jumped back. That tanned face with its mess of dark hair stared back at him, split by a huge grin that bared uneven, yellowed teeth with fibres of meat caught between them. The two canines were filed unevenly to jagged points.

'Jeez, man, don't do that!' Finn shouted. 'How did you even get here?' He pushed the window open, nearly knocking Lorenzo to the ground.

'You have plants. I climb. I listen your music. You need to meet my friend. He like music.'

'You have a friend? Is he a total weirdo, too?'

'Your music – you be successful, yes?'

'I hope so. You don't like it, do you?'

'I not like, but successful.'

'Right. Why do you think so?'

'Is bad.'

'Bad? Get lost!'

'No, is bad words – about bad stuff. People like that. But Mr Ignace will not like. You have to do deal.'

'Yes, we need a recording deal. We've put it on YouTube. Do you know what that is? Hey, why am I even talking to you?'

'Eez not allowed for you to be famous. Mister Ignace will be cross.'

'Mr Ignace can go stick it! This is all I've ever

wanted. I'm not giving it up now because of some jumped-up, '*I'm-in-charge*' vampire.'

Lorenzo climbed over the windowsill.

'Hey, what are you doing? You can't come in my house! What if my mam comes in and finds a crazy, half-naked vampire in here?'

Lorenzo shrugged.

'You don't look like person who has trouble with mother in room. This is deal ... '

'I'm not doing a deal with you! Get out of my bedroom. What are you even doing here? Why can't you stay in Hungary or wherever and use iVamp like everyone else?'

'I not use iVamp. No computer. So I am here. I help you here.'

'I don't need or want your help. And I certainly don't want you in my room. Out! Now!'

'Wait. Can I see? On YouTube?'

'Really?'

Finn flipped open the laptop. Fifteen hundred hits. It had only been – what? fifteen minutes? He clicked through the comments – people really liked it! He hit *Play* and Lorenzo watched, his face intent.

'Eez good. I like. But change key after bar eighteen – E minor better. Mr Ignace will not like video.'

'What?' Finn stared at him. 'You – are you serious? Can you play?'

'Not guitar. But I know music. You meet my

friend. He help. Yes?'

Finn shrugged.

'Why not?'

'OK. You come to Eastbourne – '

'Hang on! I can't go to Eastbourne, wherever that is. I have to go to college, I can't just disappear off somewhere. And I don't have any money.'

'I bring him here. You wait. A few days. You see him. OK?'

'Whatever. But now – out!'

five

Finn couldn't keep off the computer. He watched in amazement as the video went viral. From 1,500 hits it went to 3,000, then 10,000, then 120,000 in the first twenty-four hours.

Suddenly, it was all over the place. He was dazed, and walked around in a fug of disbelief. How had this happened?

Three days passed. The band met, but Ellie kept

her distance a bit. They practised every day.

Finn had written another song and they learned that. It was like *Life Sucks* – dark, angry, vampiric. Minor chords clashed against each other, the key changed every few bars, even within a bar. It set their teeth on edge and was hard to perform. They ended each session unsettled, but fired with excitement. It was a sound that would sell. A sound that was selling already. Gray had pulled the full version of *Life Sucks* from YouTube and put up half of it, with a link to buy the track. The new song was at least as good.

'What about a video for the new one?' asked Gray. Ellie looked away, uncomfortable. Scared, maybe. Finn touched her shoulder and she flinched.

'It's just an act. I'm sorry I scared you. You'll know, next time. I'm not going to hurt you.'

'No, Finn, I don't know. It really felt – awkward. And Todd said – '

'Don't listen to your brother! What does he know?' Finn turned away, angry, and hit a loud chord.

* * * * *

Saturday. They could practise all day and get some ideas for the video. Finn was working like a demon, inspired, driven by the songs welling up inside him. He was driving the others, too, harder than they liked. He made them practise till their fingers were raw, till their voices were hoarse, and then still keep going.

'We're riding the wave,' he said. 'We're on the brink – this is it. You've got to give 200%.' His enthusiasm fired them all.

It was cold outside. With his guitar slung over his back, Finn hurried to Iman's house where they practised in the garage.

Part way through the morning, when their energy had finally warmed the freezing space, they took a break. Finn checked his phone. There was a message and a voicemail.

He opened the message:

'Seen your video – ace stuff. Ignace will be after you! Good luck, mate – Omar.'

'Like I care,' Finn mumbled. He listened to the voicemail.

'This is Luke Secchia. I'm with Darcy and Egon. You might've heard of us. We represent Dot Comm, Grapes in a Bag, JJ Sharq. I'd like to talk to you – call me back?'

'Guys! Dot Comm's agent wants to talk to us!' He high-fived Gray. Ellie shrieked and jumped in the air.

'Call him!'

'OK, then – shut up so I can.'

They all watched, scanning Finn's face for clues, until he said 'No way! Sure, come and meet us.' He looked at the band, gave a thumbs-up sign and grinned.

'What? A gig! Yes, well ... Yes, of course. Love to!'

When he hung up, he punched the air.

'We have a gig, guys – a big one! JJ Sharq have pulled out of their set at the Farside Festival this weekend – they want us to play instead!'

They went back to practising, fired up and feverish with excitement, bouncing off each other. They played on and on, until long after dark.

The next day, Luke Secchia came and they got lunch from the chip van to celebrate – chips, curry sauce, sausages in batter. For the gig, they'd do a set of three songs. One had to be *Life Sucks*. One would be the new song they were working up. Luke was enthusiastic, waving his hands around and making promises of fame, but he didn't like their earlier songs.

'Any more like the new stuff? Doesn't matter how raw. It has – power. It's original. I love this vampire stuff. It really turns people on.'

'Maybe Finn can come up with something?' Gray said.

'Yeah, hope so. Whatever. But definitely both new ones, OK? We can cut the set to two if we have to.

'And you,' he said to Ellie, 'you were great in that video. We need that on stage. Some of that terror. You could be an actress – but don't be. I want you in this band!'

Ellie opened her mouth to complain, but Gray silenced her with a shake of his head.

'Maybe at the end of the set,' Luke went on, 'you could bite her, like you did in the video. And the guy with the crucifix could fight you off. The crowd would love it!'

'But we wouldn't,' said Finn. The memory of the crucifix was fresh and painful: why had it made him so uncomfortable? He just *knew* it would burn him. All those stories of hell-fire from his mam, no doubt – but he didn't buy that stuff. And if vampirism was a disease, surely the crucifix thing was nonsense?

He'd have to ask Ignace. But then, he didn't want anything to do with Ignace.

'Sometimes you have to suffer for your art, guys.' Luke gave a slimy smirk, and Finn tensed against him. But they needed this deal, needed Luke.

'We'll do it,' Ellie said, looking quickly at Finn. 'It will be fine.'

Six

The week was a whirlwind of practising and enjoying the heady thrill of watching their YouTube hits rocket. By Wednesday they were the 'exciting new YouTube phenomenon' and stills from their video were all over the web.

Wednesday night, Finn heard tapping at the window again. Opening it let in a cold blast of autumn wind and a few dry leaves.

'This isn't the best way of getting in touch, you know.'

'You in big trouble with Mr Ignace,' Lorenzo said.

'I don't care, OK? It's none of his business. Now go away.'

'But, Mr Finn, ... '

'No. Go away.' He slammed the window and drew the curtains closed. Half an hour later, when he peeked through the curtains, the garden was still. A dark figure stood on the path the other side of the low wall. It wasn't Lorenzo.

* * * * *

On Friday they rehearsed their stage act. Finn and Ellie acted out a biting scene, but it was feeble.

'C'mon guys, put some passion into it!' Gray shouted. 'Look like you mean it! He lifted the crucifix and waved it in Finn's direction. Finn backed off immediately.

'OK, OK – I'm not going to hit you! But, yes, that was better! Do it all like that.' They tried again, but it was no good.

'Finn,' Ellie said at last. 'You terrified me last time. What does it take to make you like that again?' No answer. 'Blood?' she whispered. Finn didn't dare move.

'All right, let's call it a day. That's not going to get any better,' Gray said at last. 'Maybe the thrill of being on stage will do it for you. I sure as hell hope so.'

* * * * *

It was dark already. Finn walked alone, the fog curling around him.

'Wait up. Vampire boy.' Finn froze. 'Don't mess with my sister. Wasn't breaking her heart enough for you?' Todd was blocking his path.

'I didn't mean to upset her. The biting, it was just the video.'

'That wasn't acting. You told her you were a vampire.'

'It's in the song – that's all.'

'You got off on biting her, on her bleeding. Keep away, weirdo.' Todd raised his arm, a solid shadow in the gloom.

Finn's fists came up, too.

Instantly a figure appeared behind Todd, jumping around nervously. Black hair, wet with fog, hung in ropes.

'No, no, Mr Finn. Not hit heem!'

Todd spun round.

'I'm no wuss. I'll hit him if I want to!' Finn snapped at Lorenzo.

'This hobo your minder, is he?' laughed Todd.

'No, no,' Lorenzo was still jiggling. 'Eez very bad if he bleed. You take capsule, then you hit him.'

Finn stopped, fist in mid-air. It was true. He'd grown up fighting – as a skinny, ginger, Irish kid in England he'd had to. But how could he fight if blood turned him mad with desire?

That pause was all Todd needed. In a moment, the blade of his knife flashed in front of Finn, then glinted across the back of Finn's fist. He felt it chink against the bone, and pulled his hand back, fast.

They all stared at Finn's hand. The edges of the wound gaped, but the blood didn't flow. At last it crept up – but so slowly. *Time slows down in an emergency*, thought Finn. But the blood really wasn't coming. Todd couldn't tear his eyes from the wound. He looked scared now.

'What's wrong with you?' he shouted. 'You freak! You get off on biting my sister, and you don't bleed! What are you?'

Pause.

'Oh. Oh my God.' Todd stepped back, away from Finn, his eyes wide.

'Scared now, are you?' Finn sneered. Todd took another step backwards.

'This is insane. There's no such thing. It's ... '

'You sure?' Finn menaced, grinning, ignoring the pain in his hand. Lorenzo was still hopping about.

'No, Mr Feenn. Please. Take capsule.'

Finn took the ProVamp from his pocket and swallowed it.

'Now I can hit you. Or perhaps I should just bite you?'

Todd backed away. 'Keep away from my sister, right? I'm watching you.'

'Yeah, from a distance,' laughed Finn and faked a lunge at him. Todd turned and ran.

Seven

Saturday came and they piled into the van Luke had arranged. Their gig was in the evening, so they sound-checked early and had all day to listen to other bands before their turn came.

There was some grumbling from the punters that JJ Sharq had cancelled, and Finn wondered if it would turn nasty, but as they filed onto the stage the crowd cheered Finn's vampire cloak.

Finn played the first few chords and everyone fell silent. Soon the music took over and they all forgot their worries and played as well as they ever had, perhaps better.

They saved *Life Sucks* until last. As they paused, Finn took a gulp of water, but left the ProVamp capsule in his pocket. Their rehearsals had been pitifully unconvincing, and he needed the spice of possibility. He couldn't afford to dull his desire.

They played, he sang, the crowd danced and it was everything he had ever wanted it to be.

'*Suck my blood*,' he sang straight at Ellie, looking into her eyes. Perhaps he did still want her after all. She was hot in her short, black skirt and her ripped tights, her thick eyeliner and her blood-red lipstick. He felt a stirring inside him.

'I'll suck yours ...'

And he caught her by the neck and dragged her to his mouth. It was more this time, more than in rehearsal. Something was different. Something was real again, like the first time. His mouth was at her neck and he could smell blood, taste it in the air like a shark is supposed to be able to taste it in the water from three miles away. Where was she bleeding? He ran his hands over her arms and felt her shiver beneath his fingers. He could tell she wanted him, too.

He started to bite, nibble at first, but then really bite. She moaned, but it quickly changed to a scream. And then Gray was coming at him waving the crucifix, and the terror of burning snatched away the taste of blood.

Finn pushed Ellie off as if she was poison. The hurt on her face was as real as the terror. Finn was furious with Gray and snarled at him even as he backed away – but Gray winked at him, still thinking he was acting. And then the lights went out and the crowd roared.

'Get off the stage!' whispered Gray. 'They need us out of the way for the next act!'

He tried to drag Finn, who had let go of Ellie but was standing frozen. Ellie fled to the back of the stage. Finn shook Gray off.

'Keep that thing away from me!' he snapped.

'OK, mate, calm down. What's the problem? Sorry if it's the Catholic thing. No offense – it's just, well, anti-vampire.'

Finn's face was white, but in the low light it didn't matter. He'd got away with it. But then a firm hand gripped his shoulder and spun him round.

'What are you playing at? I told you to leave her alone.' It was Todd.

Still shaken, Finn was defensive.

'I didn't want to do that stuff – Ellie did!'

'Don't give me that! She was dead scared.'

Finn's anger rose through his fear.

'Your sister's in the band, and this is our gig. If she doesn't like it, she needs to talk to us, not you. Now, get out of here!' and he pushed Todd away.

Todd raised his fists, but a security guard grabbed his arms from behind.

'Away from the stage, mate. None of that here.'

Todd glowered at Finn across the space opening between them. The roar of applause subsided and the crowd shuffled, as some people left the tent and others made their way in.

'I'll stake you if I have to!' Todd shouted.

'Finn.'

It was a low, calm voice – a voice he hadn't wanted to hear again: Ignace.

Finn ignored him and followed the band into the green room. They shared some cans and buzzed with excitement. Luke hovered around, flapping his arms and talking enthusiastically. Gray worked at including him, but Finn was still shaken – he had no time for Luke.

What had happened? Why had he felt that rush of hunger for her blood this time? It worried him. And Todd. Todd didn't scare him, but that threat of staking – Todd really did believe he was a vampire. It would be great publicity if that rumour got going, and Finn was not one to take any notice of Ignace's stupid rules.

But a vampire is a challenge. If people believed it, he'd be followed around by weirdos and yes, perhaps some of them really would want to stake him. Ignace would probably be relieved if Finn got staked – but it was something to think about.

He looked across at Ellie. She'd been subdued at first, but now she was fizzing with excitement. She had a drink in one hand and was running the other hand through her hair. She did look hot. And not just blood-hot to the vampire in him.

Eight

Half an hour later they all wandered out for something to eat.

'Can we get burgers?' Ellie asked.

'Get anything – my treat,' said Luke.

'Steak sandwich?' Finn asked.

'Sure.'

'I'll have it extra rare,' Finn said.

'Still in vampire mode, mate?' Gray smiled at him and Finn laughed.

'Yeah, good bit of bloody meat. It'll keep my mind off biting Ellie.'

They all laughed, Ellie loudest. Todd's face flicked through Finn's mind.

Finn ate the steak and ditched as much of the bread roll as he could. No one noticed. They were used to him eating nothing when they went out. He always said he wasn't hungry, but really he couldn't afford the burgers and chips and drinks they bought. And now Luke was paying, Finn was a vampire and couldn't eat most of that stuff anyway. Typical of his luck.

* * * * *

As Finn piled the last of the stuff into the van, fog gathered around the street lamps. Finn was aware of shapes in the gloom. Not just people walking past, but someone hanging around – at least one person, maybe more. He shivered and hugged his arms around his skinny body, then slammed the back door of the van and started to walk away.

'Stop right there.'

Finn sighed, weary, not wanting confrontation.

'Know what this is?' Todd raised his arms and Finn saw he was carrying a sharpened wooden stick. 'It's a stake. Know what it's for?'

'Are you crazy?' Finn snapped. 'You don't really believe in vampires do you, jerk?'

Todd raised the stake, jabbing the sharp end

towards Finn, who took a step backwards.

'Scared, vampire boy?'

'You find someone who doesn't back away from a sharp stick! You don't have to be a vampire not to want to be stabbed!'

Todd laughed. 'But it helps, doesn't it?'

Two more figures grew out of the fog and stood beside Todd. One raised a hand in greeting.

'Vampire boy.'

This was going to get ugly. Finn stuffed a ProVamp capsule in his mouth. If there was going to be blood, he was going to be ready for it.

'Keep away from my sister,' Todd snarled. Finn waited for the lunge, but it didn't come. He felt a slight warmth at his back, as though there was someone behind him, cutting the wind. He didn't dare turn, he couldn't afford to take his eyes off Todd and his gang. But whoever was behind him, Todd had seen them and that's why he held the stake still. Finn put his tongue between his lips, thinking.

'If I'm a vampire,' he said, 'what's to stop me just biting you – or your pretty sister?' He was goading Todd – it was dangerous – but this had to stop.

'This is.' Todd shook the stake.

'Hah! You've got to get me to lie down first! I'm not going down without a fight. One bite!'

He bared his teeth at Todd. It was a joke, the movie-vampire pose he'd done on stage, but it was enough for the man behind him, who now laid a hand on his shoulder.

'Enough, Finn.' It was Ignace.

Finn's instinct was to shake him off, but he didn't. He stood still, with Ignace's hand on his shoulder, and stared at Todd.

'Who's your creepy friend?' Todd asked.

'Go home, little boy,' Ignace said.

Furious, Todd ran at them both with the stake. Finn broke free from Ignace. He grabbed Todd's arm and twisted it hard so that he cried out, but he didn't drop the stake.

'Let go of me, you freak!' shouted Todd. But Finn was by far the stronger. He hauled Todd's arm towards his mouth.

'Who's scared now, eh?' he said, smiling, showing his teeth. Todd struggled, but it was no use. The other two stood frozen, staring.

Finn moved his mouth closer, making Todd frantic.

'Finn, stop it!' commanded Ignace.

But Finn took no notice. His teeth grazed Todd's skin. Suddenly, despite the ProVamp, he wanted nothing more than to sink his teeth deep into the flesh and feel the hot blood flood his mouth. He wasn't even going to struggle against it. He felt weak with desire for it. Desire – for a boy! Part of him recoiled, part was interested – most didn't care; it just ached with wanting.

But then everything was shattered. It was as though the sky broke apart into a thousand tiny fragments and they rained down around him. Finn had to look at them. There they were, scattered in the mud. Tiny, white grains. He had to look at them, had to know how many there were. It was a desire even stronger than the hunger for blood. He dropped Todd's arm and fell to his knees.

'What the ... ?' Todd sprang back and looked in astonishment at Finn kneeling in the mud clutching at grains of rice. 'What's going on?'

'Rice,' Ignace said. 'Just rice. But he's ... allergic. Now run, you fool. He's much stronger than you and your gang of babies. Run! I'll give you five seconds. One ... two ... three ... '

Todd looked at his companions, began to laugh, then thought better of it. He held up his hands to Ignace and turned.

'OK, we're going. Freak. Freak and vampire boy. But this isn't the end of it.'

'It is for tonight,' said Ignace. 'Four ... five ... three hundred and ninety six.' They had gone. The field was still, except for Ignace standing over Finn, who was still scrabbling in the mud. 'You can stop now, Finn. There's three hundred and ninety six, as I said. Stand up.'

Finn stood. He felt drained and shaky. 'What happened?'

'You had to count them. It's an old Eastern European trick to stop vampires: throwing millet, or rice, or corn. We're compelled to count things; can't pass them until we know how many grains there are.' He paused. 'So don't go on the beach.'

'That's crazy! Why aren't you counting them?'

'I know how many there are. I already counted them.'

Nine

Ignace looked hard at Finn, who fidgeted uncomfortably and angrily.

'This has to stop.'

'No,' Finn said. 'This isn't going to stop. This is all I ever wanted, to make it with my music. I'm not stopping – not for you or for anyone.'

'You can't be famous. And you certainly can't go around claiming to be a vampire!'

'Why not? I *am* a vampire. And it sure as hell sells,' Finn shouted.

'But if people believe it – and Todd obviously believes it – there's trouble. Big trouble. When people believe in vampires they try to destroy them. They look for us – and they find us. There will be a massacre. You're playing a dangerous game and I can't allow it to go on.'

'*You* can't allow it? Since when do you tell me what to do? I'll do whatever I like and you can't stop me,' Finn shouted.

He was about to stomp off, but thought better of it. Best not to look like a stroppy teen.

'I need to get out of this hole I live in. Have you seen it? It's all right for you with your castle and your lake and your little islands. This is the real world. I live in a dump – a council hovel with my mam and my stupid sister and whichever half-wit boyfriend my mam brings home for a few months. We eat junk; we can't afford to do anything. And I'm not staying like this. Music is my ticket out and I'm not giving it up for anything. You can't make me.'

Ignace waited, silent and calm, which made Finn feel foolish, and that made him fidget more, and that made him feel more foolish.

'I can stop you, as you well know. But it would be better if I didn't have to.'

He dropped a few grains of rice to the floor from his pocket and Finn felt the overwhelming urge to count them.

'Don't bother,' said Ignace. 'Thirty-seven.'

'Why does that happen?' Finn hated to have to ask Ignace anything, but there was no other way to know.

'It's part of the disease – arithmomania, the need to count things. It's been used against us for centuries. It's why people throw rice and confetti at weddings – to keep us away. So don't go to any weddings or you'll look a total fool.

'I'll do a deal with you,' Ignace offered at last. 'One year. You can have a year as a star and we'll review it. But lay off the '*I'm a vampire*' stuff.'

'No. A year's not enough. Five years.'

Ignace raised an eyebrow.

'You want to bargain with me? Are you aware who I am?'

'Do I care?'

Ignace smiled.

'You will either take my deal or I will destroy your 'career' right now,' he said.

'You can't take away all I've ever wanted or worked for just to defend yourself and your cronies,' Finn shouted.

Ignace brought his fingertips together as he thought.

'I know it's hard for you to see why this is how it must be. Which is why –'

Finn clenched his fists.

'How dare you?!' he shouted. 'Who are you to boss me around?'

'Well, let's see ... '

Ignace gave a wry smile. It was the wrong thing to do. Finn lunged at him, fists flailing. Ignace stepped quickly aside and Finn fell, sprawling on the ground.

'Calm down. A year; then you're mine. Think about it.'

'No way!'

Ignace tossed a handful of rice at Finn and walked into the night.

Ten

'You come out now? Meet my friend in bar?' Lorenzo asked through the closed window.

Finn ignored him. He lay on his bed, listening on his headphones to the recording of their newest song.

Lorenzo rapped loudly on the glass.

'Get lost!' Finn shouted. 'You can go to hell, the lot of you!'

'Oh, Mr Feenn, I'm not here for Mr Ignace – I'm here for you. My friend – he teach you better music, yes? He is here now. He not like Mr Ignace either. Come to the bar, come now.'

Finn pulled back the curtain and opened the window, but Lorenzo had gone, scrambling down the creeper and running across the lawn.

Finn grabbed a hoodie and loped down the stairs. He wasn't expecting anything of this meeting. What did he need? He had fans, he had a deal, he had what that bozo Luke would call a USP – a *unique selling proposition*: he was the only real vampire on YouTube.

Drizzle spattered the street and formed a mist over Finn's clothes. The warm air of the bar rushed out to draw him in as he opened the door.

He pushed a hand through his damp hair, walked in and looked around. The smoke-stained walls hadn't been cleaned since smoking had been banned, the tables were scarred and the fake leather of the seat covers was cracked and torn.

Lorenzo sat in a corner beside a chubby man with black hair. The man was staring into a pint glass, clutched between hands studded with signet rings. He didn't look up as Finn pulled out a stool and sat down. Neither of them offered to buy him a drink.

'I saw your video,' the chubby man said. His hair was too dark, dyed black when it should be showing lines of grey, and it was gelled or sprayed into a tacky, puffy style. His voice had an American drawl. There was something slightly familiar about him.

'Have I seen you before?' Finn asked.

'Doubt it. I work in a chip shop. Not near here – in Eastbourne. Your voice is good. Your guitar – well, it's a train wreck. Music's gotta make ya move. You're not there yet. You gotta work the tune, dude.'

Finn bristled.

'Yeah? What's wrong with it? Details?'

'Details? Huh! What do I know about music? You don't need to know too much about music in this business, you just need to feel it. You can do better. It's gotta be drama – it's gotta be wild. You need more passion.'

'I *do* know you, don't I?' Finn said, peering at the man.

'I don't think so.'

'Hey! You're – '

The man held his gaze, half-smiled.

'Yeah?' he said.

'You're Elvis. Elvis Presley.'

'Yeah. You're right. I *am* Elvis Presley. But there ain't nobody gonna believe you, so don't bother sayin' it.'

Finn stared at Elvis. Being a vampire was weird enough. Being a vampire in a dingy pub in north London with Elvis Presley was enough to weird anyone out.

'So all the stuff about 'Elvis isn't really dead' – it's true then?'

'Yep. But not all of it. There's a load of nutters about, you know? It's not like everyone has seen me.'

'So what happened?'

'I got vamped. A vampire can't stay famous *and* alive, as you're about to find out, man.'

'I'm going to be famous whatever Ignace says.'

'Won't happen. See, thing is, if you're famous, and you never age, someone's gonna notice some time. And Ignace's boys, they're scared of that.'

'I'll say I had botox. And facelifts. Whatever. It doesn't matter.'

'Eet does matter. Mr Ignace not allow. You must do deal with Mr Ignace,' Lorenzo added. Finn had forgotten he was there.

'Mr Ignace will have no freakin' say in it!'

'You do deal, like with devil. You have success now, he have your soul later,' Lorenzo went on.

'Look,' said Elvis. 'I 'died' at forty-two. And I don't look much different now, right? D'you think people gonna believe Elvis looks the same at eighty as at forty? Hey, how about a hundred? What about when I'm still pulling chicks at two hundred?'

'But everyone knows you weren't born hundreds of years ago like Ignace, or mad Lorenzo here,' said Finn.

'I was vamped in the '70s. Being a vampire and being *that* famous – it's not cool.'

'How did you – you know – get vamped?'

'Don't go with the chicks that follow the band – you don't know where they've been or what they are. One bite is all it takes.'

'I thought we weren't allowed to bite people?'

'And like we all do as we're told? Come on, kid – I was a trophy vampire!'

He snorted with laughter and his drink slopped in its glass.

'She bit me so she could say 'I turned Elvis Presley into a vampire,' just like they'll go with you so they can say 'I did it with Finn.' Ignace's boys soon taught her a lesson, eh Lorenzo?'

Lorenzo shuddered.

'Look,' Elvis went on, 'I'll teach you to work an audience, drive them wild, like you'd drive a '67

Mustang, and you'll be famous, I swear. But after three years, you vanish. You can 'die' or disappear or retire – it don't matter how – but you go. You can have everything you want, you can rule the world – but not for long. And don't bug Ignace – you ain't gonna win.'

'And if I refuse?'

'I go back to the chip shop and you put cruddy videos on YouTube for a few weeks and poof! you vanish back into the crowd of losers.'

Finn bristled again. 'And if I can do it on my own?'

'What makes you think you can?'

'What makes you think I can't?'

'Your call. With me, it's guaranteed. Or you can

take your chance like the other two-bit punks. And hey – you can practise for four hundred years if you need to, if you ain't good enough. No rush. You got plenty of time.

'Up for it then, kid? Deal or no deal?'

'Deal,' said Finn.

'Sign in blood.'

Elvis pushed a piece of paper towards Finn.

'What?'

'Just kidding. Now – where's your guitar? Let's get going, man!'

THE HENLEY COLLEGE LIBRARY

Vampire Dawn

The story starts with **Die Now or Live Forever**. Read it first.

Then follow each individual's story. You can read these in any order:

Juliette's story

Finn's story

Omar's story

Alistair and Ruby's story

Ava's story

Plus an essential guide for new vampires.

Find out more at www.vampiredawn.co.uk. Follow the vampires on Facebook: www.facebook.com/VampireDawnBooks

twitter: @vampiredawn